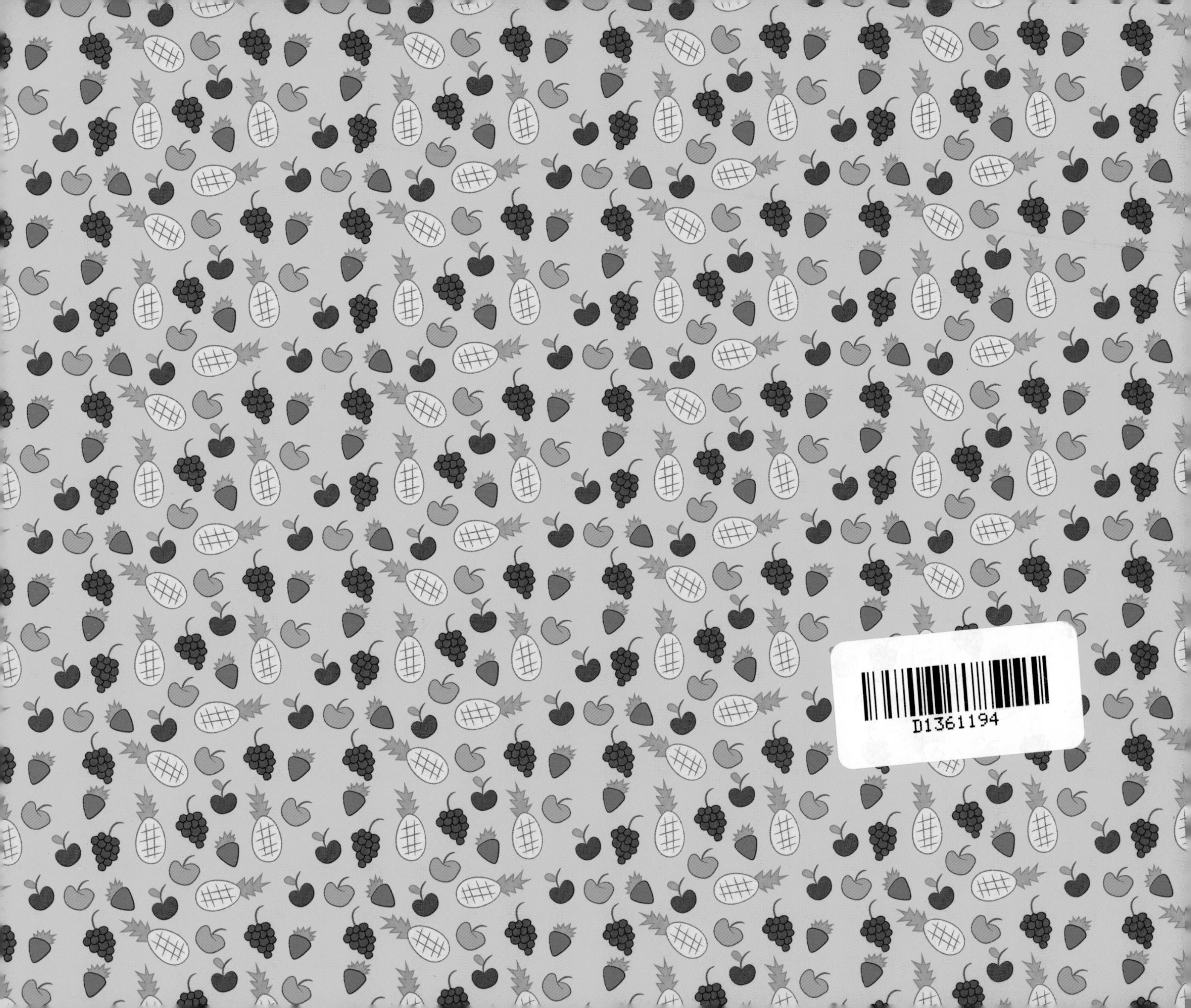

Published by
Vegan Publishers
Danvers, MA
www.veganpublishers.com

Cover art and design by Carlos Patiño
Book design by Carlos Patiño

Vegan carrot cake recipe by Natalie Slater, creator of BakeandDestroy.com

ISBN: 978-1-940184-00-5
Library of Congress Control Number: 2014937536

Printed and bound by Tien Wah Press (Pte) Ltd, May 2014, in Malaysia

Lena of Vegitopia

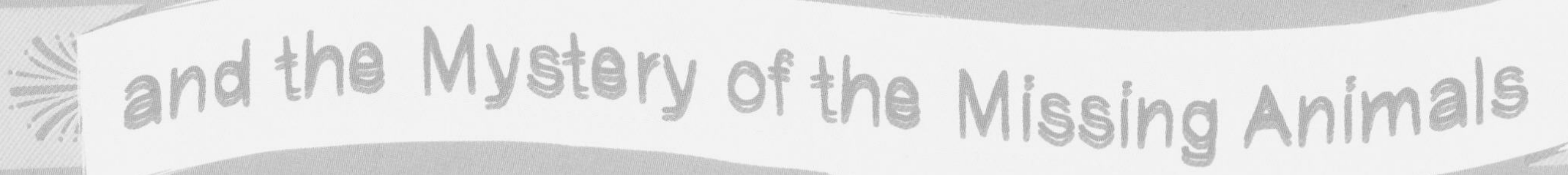

By Sybil Severin
Illustrated by Carlos Patiño

Did you know that there is a place
where humans and other animals live
together in peace?

This place is called Vegitopia, and if you were ever to suggest that anyone in the great Kingdom of Vegitopia eat animals, they would think you were crazy! In Vegitopia, all animals are friends, not food.

One of these friends is a special cow named Flora. Flora lives next to a sweet girl named Lena Lentil Beans. Lena has her own lettuce patch, and Flora likes to visit Lena and munch on the tasty lettuce that she grows.

One day, Lena was out tending her lettuce patch when she heard a sad, whimpering sound. It was Flora! The gentle cow was crying by the far end of the patch.

"Flora! What's wrong?" asked Lena. "Oh Lena," said Flora, "you have to help me. One of my babies has gone missing."

"Don't worry. I'll help you find her," Lena replied as she immediately began to put away her garden tools. Soon, the two friends were off in the fields searching for Flora's dear baby. In a short time, they came upon a group of pigs and decided to ask them if they had seen the little calf.

Several of the pigs looked frightened. They told Lena that some of their piglets had gone missing during the night. It wasn't just the pigs who were upset; mother hens had woken up to find their babies missing as well. Even the baby fish had been taken right out of the water in Vegitopia's peaceful ponds.

Lena was puzzled. Why would baby animals suddenly go missing in Vegitopia? It was quite a mystery all right, but Lena knew that as a human in Vegitopia it was her responsibility to help protect the animals of the land. She had to figure out a way to find the animals and bring them back home to their parents, where they belonged.

That night, Lena decided to write a letter to the princess of Vegitopia, Princess Vegi-Terry-Anne, asking her for help in finding the missing babies. Lena just knew that the princess would be able to help.

In a few short days, a letter addressed to Lena came via the Royal Vegi–Post. By that time, more baby animals had gone missing, and Lena was becoming very anxious. This is what the letter said:

DEAR LENA,

I'M SO GLAD YOU HAVE INFORMED ME OF THE TERRIBLE INJUSTICE GOING ON RIGHT HERE IN OUR PEACEFUL KINGDOM OF VEGITOPIA. I KNOW EXACTLY WHO IS RESPONSIBLE FOR THE MISSING BABIES. HER NAME IS CARNISTA, AND SHE RAN AWAY FROM VEGITOPIA A LONG TIME AGO BECAUSE SHE REFUSED TO EAT ANY FRUITS OR VEGETABLES. SHE ABSOLUTELY HATES THEM! NOW SHE LIVES ALONE IN AN OLD CASTLE ON THE OUTSKIRTS OF THE KINGDOM. WE NEED TO GO TO HER CASTLE AND RESCUE THE BABIES BEFORE SHE CAN EAT THEM. LENA, YOU ARE A BRAVE GIRL FOR STANDING UP FOR THE ANIMALS OF VEGITOPIA. I KNOW THAT TOGETHER WE WILL BE ABLE TO RETURN THE BABIES TO THEIR HOMES SAFELY.

SINCERELY,

PRINCESS VEGI-TERRY-ANNE

Lena was stunned. She could hardly believe that the princess of Vegitopia would be coming to her humble little lettuce patch!

When Princess Vegi-Terry-Anne arrived at Lena's lettuce patch, she was greeted by all of the kind animals who lived nearby. Lena offered her finest head of lettuce to the princess and admired her beautiful wand that had a single, perfect daisy blossoming from the end of it.

"Thank you, Lena," said the princess as she took a bite. "Your lettuce is the most fresh and crisp in all the land! I wish I had time to eat more, but we really must hurry. Carnista's castle is all the way at the edge of Vegitopia, and we have no time to waste."

After saying goodbye to the animals, Lena tucked a piece of carrot cake into her pocket for the journey, and she and the princess hurried off. It was a long trek, but finally they arrived at Carnista's castle. What a ghastly sight! No fruits or vegetables or plants of any kind were growing on the land that surrounded the castle. There was thick smog in the air, and the sunlight could barely get through the dark and dirty clouds above.

"How do we get in there?" asked Lena as she peered through the wrought iron gates at the castle's entrance.

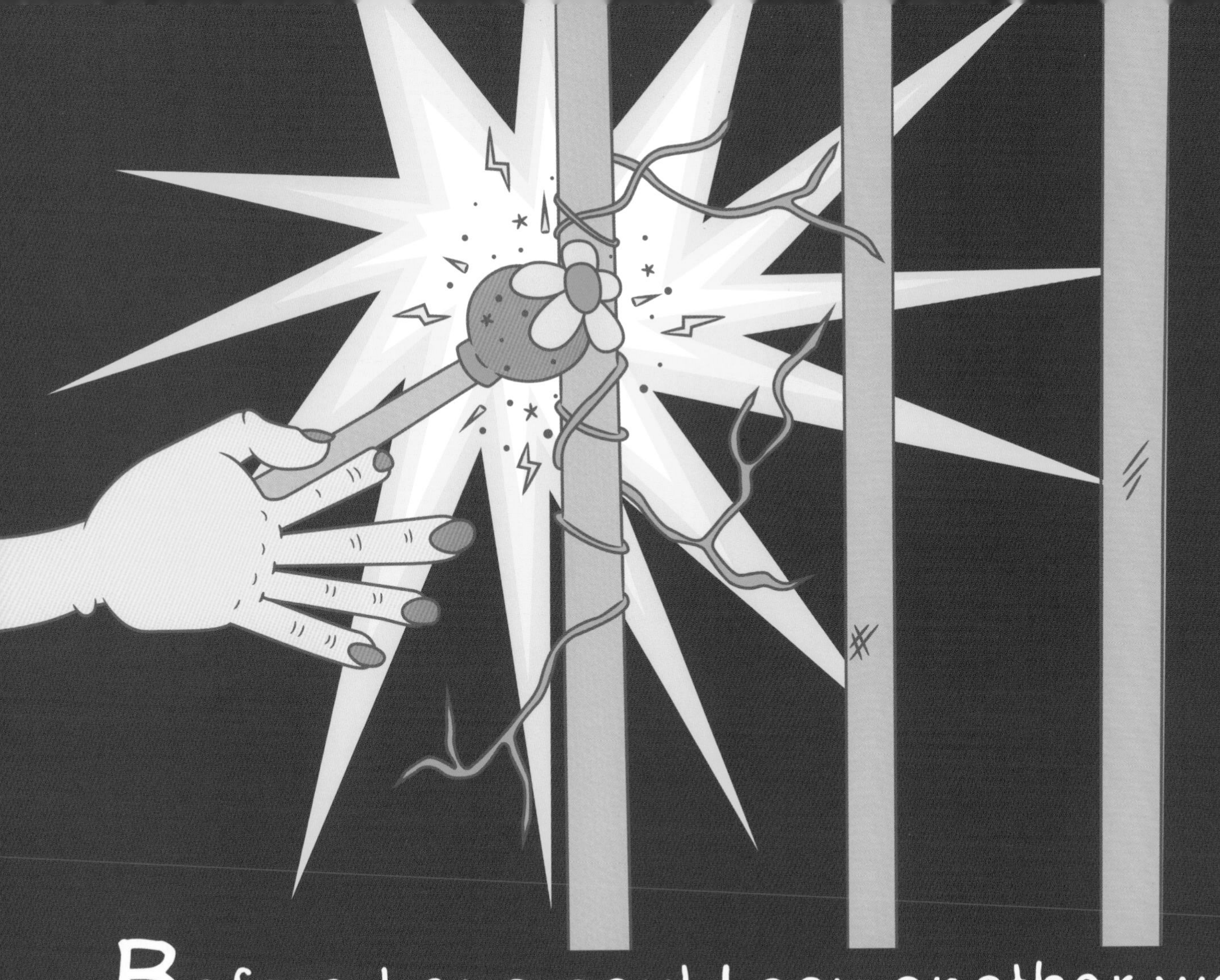

Before Lena could say another word, the princess touched her daisy wand to the gate, and suddenly vines began to grow out of thin air.

The princess scurried up the vines and gave her hand to Lena so that she could climb up as well. Lena was speechless. She wondered what other magical tricks the princess had up her sleeve.

Once they were inside the castle, they were greeted by a foul stench. Lena held her nose. She was beginning to feel scared. What if Carnista caught them? Would she lock them in her dungeon with the captured animals and cook them for dinner? She shivered at the thought and hurried to catch up to the princess as she rushed down a steep stone stairwell. When they got to the bottom, they found themselves in the very pit of Carnista's dungeon. Hundreds of baby animals pleaded for help behind bars and in cages. It was an awful sight!

"Here, you take this," said the princess as she handed Lena her wand. "Just touch the wand to each lock, and the animals will be freed. I need to go find Carnista and figure out how to unlock the main gates to the castle. I'm afraid my magic just isn't strong enough to open them!"

Lena nodded and quickly got to work unlocking each cage. The animals crowded around her, and together they all climbed out of the dungeon. They were almost at the gates when a terrifying cackle pierced the air. It was Carnista, and she was determined to stop them from escaping.

Her hair was brown and stringy, and her face was pale and wrinkly. A large stomach bulged from beneath her tattered robes.

"You can't have these animals!" shrieked Carnista. "They are my only food. You can't expect me to survive only on icky fruits and vegetables. I have an appetite, you know!"

"But fruits and vegetables aren't icky," said Lena. "They are the most natural and delicious food the world has to offer!"
"That's not true," scoffed Carnista.

Lena suddenly had an idea. She reached into her pocket, took out the carrot cake she had been saving as a snack, and handed it to Carnista.

"Just try this. I baked it myself this morning with fresh carrots from my garden."

"Is there meat in it?" asked Carnista as she inspected the cake.

"Of course not," said Lena. "There is not one single thing from an animal in that cake. It's vegan."

"Vegan!" cried Carnista, looking horrified. "I'd rather eat dogs' droppings!"

"Just try it," begged Lena, still trying to buy time as she waited for the princess to return.

Carnista sniffed the cake and gave it one tiny bite. Then, in the blink of an eye, she gobbled up the entire thing.

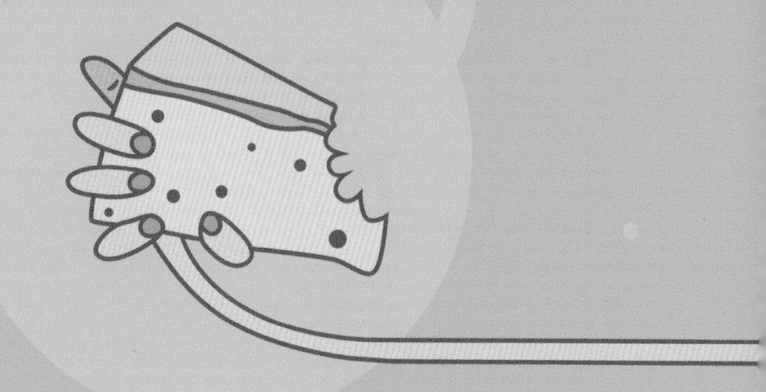

"That was... so... delicious! You must give me more of that cake."

"The rest of it is at my house. You can have some more if you just let me and these animals go home. I can even teach you how to make it," said Lena.

Just then, Princess Vegi-Terry-Anne stepped between Lena and Carnista, and with one wave of her daisy wand, she produced a huge spread of vegan treats. Carnista hungrily gobbled them up as Lena and the animals ran through the gate.

"How were you able to get the gates to open up?" Lena asked the princess as they began the journey home. "I thought you said your magic wasn't strong enough."

"It was your carrot cake, Lena. There must be something very special about the carrots you grow in your garden– perhaps they are enchanted. No one has ever gotten Carnista to look at a vegetable, let alone eat something vegan. The moment she bit into that cake, the gates just unlocked!"

Lena and the princess were happy to reunite the baby animals with their mothers and fathers, and Lena was given the special honor of Royal Vegan Baker of the Kingdom of Vegitopia.

And what, you may ask, became of Carnista? Well, after her first taste of carrot in Lena's yummy cake, Carnista decided that she would never eat meat again.

She began to grow her own vegetables, and her castle started to look a little less gloomy. Even Carnista herself didn't look so hideous anymore. Her hair became thick and shiny, and her face took on a healthy glow from gardening in the sunshine.

The smog above the castle lifted, and the foul stench went away because she no longer cooked animals for dinner.

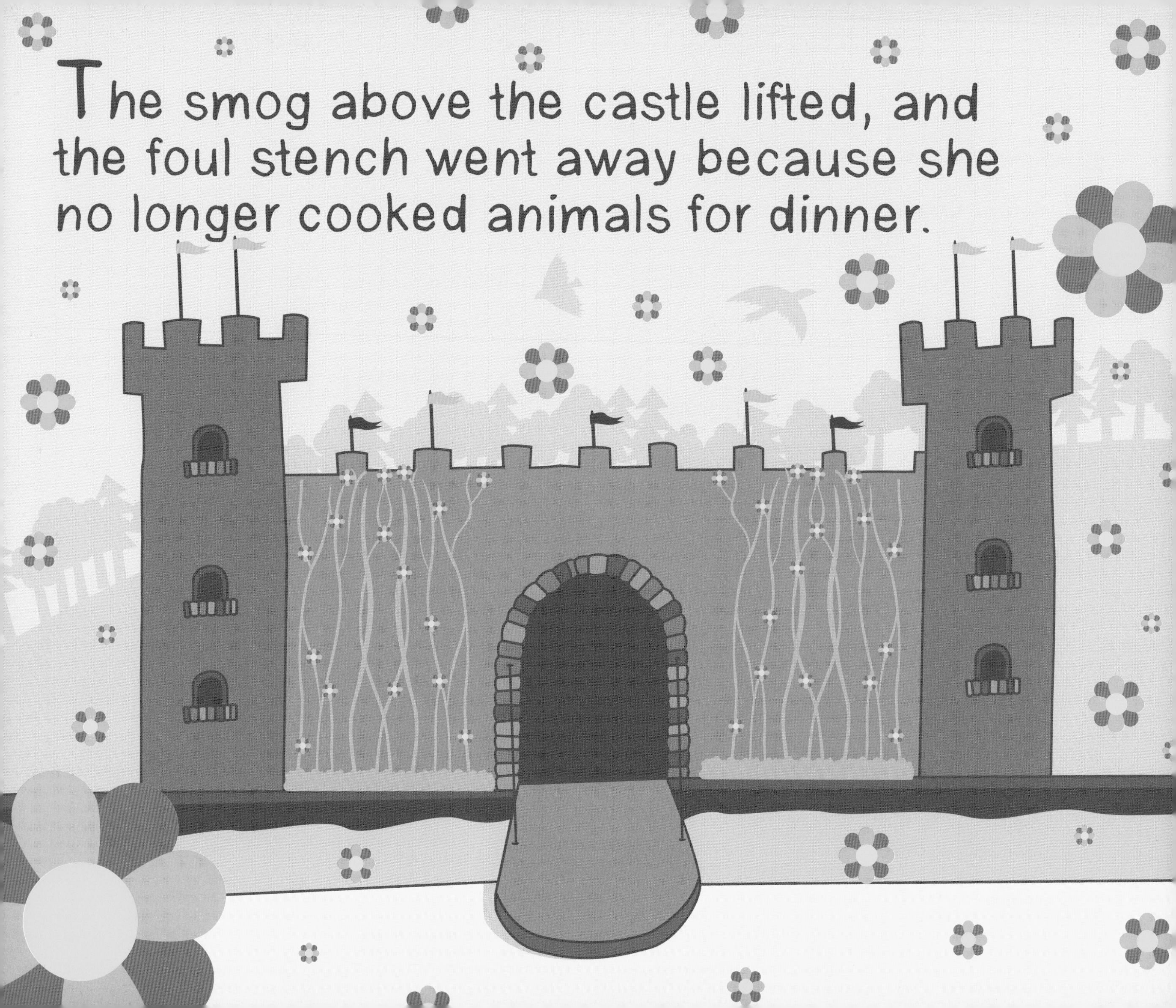

And one day, Carnista found a gift on her doorstep. When she opened up the box, she found a beautiful, green head of lettuce with a card from Lena that simply read:

LENA'S
VEGAN
CARROT CAKE

From the Royal Bakery of the Kingdom of Vegitopia
Lena's Vegan Carrot Cake

Ingredients:

- 1 & ½ cups all-purpose flour*
- 1 & ½ cups cake flour**
- 1 tablespoon baking powder
- 1 teaspoon salt
- ½ teaspoon ground allspice
- ½ teaspoon ground cinnamon
- ½ teaspoon ground nutmeg
- 1 cup plain soy milk
- 1 cup raw agave nectar
- ½ cup sweet potato puree or one mashed, overripe banana (the princess's favorite)
- 1 tablespoon vanilla
- 1 teaspoon apple cider vinegar
- 3 cups grated carrots
- 1 cup chopped pecans (optional)
- 1 cup raisins (optional)

*Sometimes Lena likes to substitute up to half this amount with whole wheat flour.
**Lena usually uses whole wheat pastry flour!

Grease two 9-inch round cake pans and preheat the oven to 350°F. Sift together the flours, baking powder, salt, allspice, cinnamon, and nutmeg. Stir in the soy milk, agave nectar, potato puree, vanilla, and vinegar until just mixed. Fold in the carrots, pecans, and raisins. Allow the batter to rest for 5 minutes before pouring into the prepared pans – you may need to spread the batter in the pan with a rubber spatula. Bake 28-31 minutes, or until the tops of the cakes spring back when lightly touched with your finger.

Lena doesn't usually put frosting on her carrot cake, but for special occasions, like when the princess comes to visit, Lena will top the cake with this yummy frosting:

- 2 cups raw cashews, soaked 4-6 hours
- 2 tablespoons lemon juice
- 2 tablespoons liquid coconut oil
- ⅓ cup maple syrup
- 1 teaspoon orange zest

Drain the cashews and place all of the ingredients in a food processor or high-speed blender. Blend until smooth – add a splash of water or soy milk if necessary for a creamy consistency. Spread evenly over cooled cake, slice, and serve!

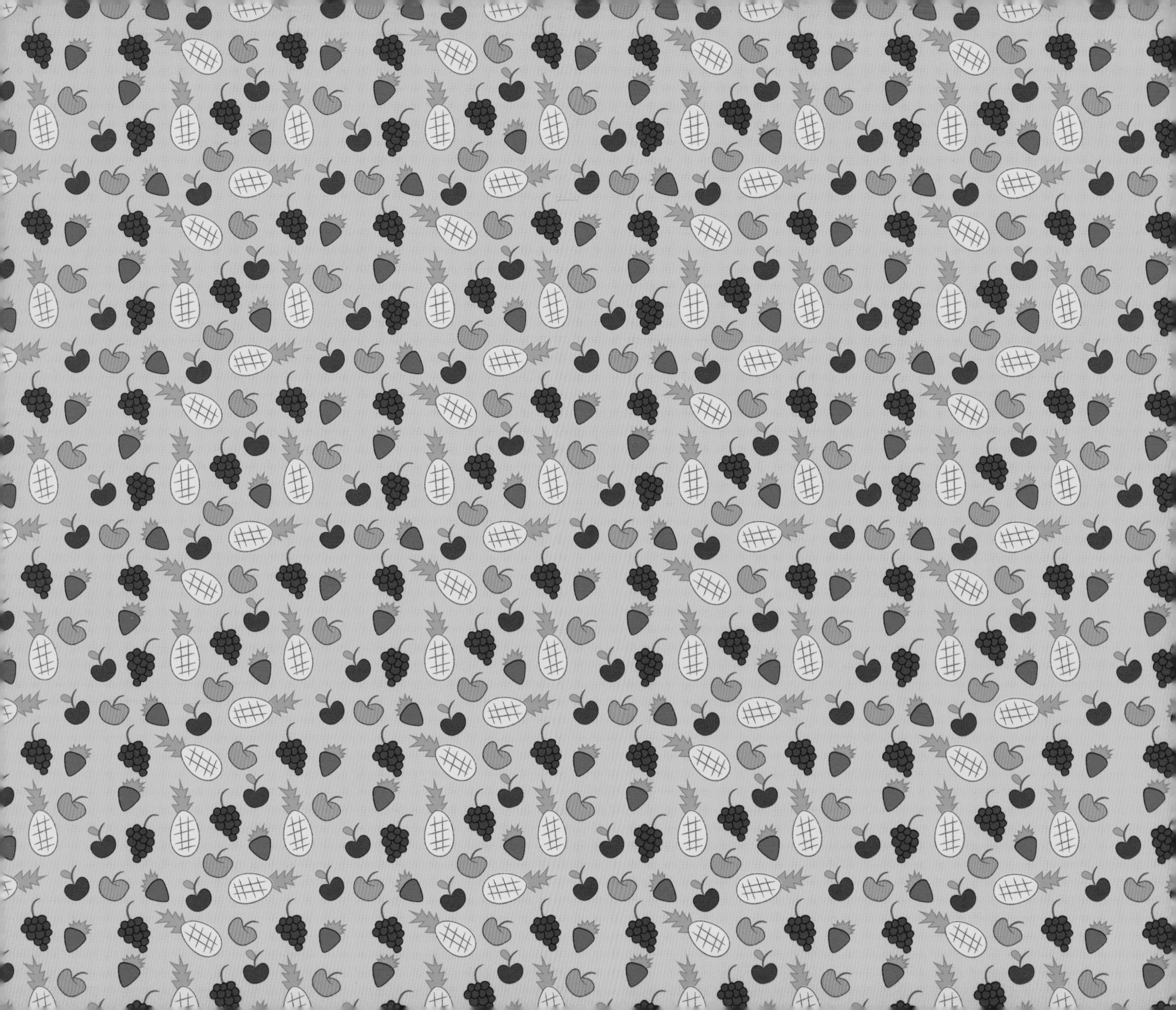